Boo!

For Jacqueline and Dominique — KH
For Kevin, the boy behind the mask — JM

Note

Once a reader can recognize and identify the thirty-three words used to tell this story, he or she will be able to successfully read the entire book. These thirty-three words are repeated throughout the story, so that young readers will be able to recognize easily the words and understand their meaning.

The thirty-three words used in this book are:

a	dog	is	one	that
and	else	mad	oops	what's
boo	fangs	me	scare	with
but	friends	mom	scary	yikes
cat	I	monster	see	you
claws	I'll	my	she's	
dad	I'm	no	teacher	

Library of Congress Cataloging-in-Publication Data

Hall, Kirsten.
    Boo! / by Kirsten Hall; illustrated by John Magine.
      p. cm. — (My first reader)
      Summary: A boy disguised as a monster scares his friend, his parents, and eventually himself.
      ISBN 0-516-05370-1
      [1. Disguise — Fiction. 2. Costume — Fiction. 3. Monsters — Fiction.] I. Magine, John, ill.
      II. Title. III. Series.
PZ7.H1457B 1995
[E] — dc20

95–10110
CIP
AC

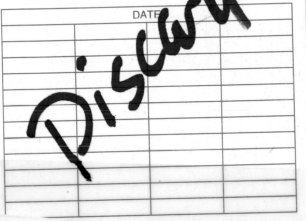

Boo!

Written by Kirsten Hall   *Illustrated by John Magine*

𝒞𝒫 Children's Press®
A Division of Grolier Publishing
New York London Hong Kong Sydney
Danbury, Connecticut

Developed by Nancy Hall, Inc. Electronic page composition by Lindaanne Donohoe Design.
1 2 3 4 5 6 7 8 9 10 R 05 04 03 02 01 00 99 98 97 96 95

I'm a scary monster!

Boo!

7

I'll scare my friends,

And I'll scare you!

I'll scare my mom,

I'll scare my dad,

I'll scare my teacher . . .

Oops! She's mad!

19

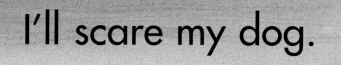
I'll scare my dog.

I'll scare my cat.

FACE PAINT

With claws, and fangs, and . . .

25

26

Yikes! What's that?!?

That scary monster that I see,

Is no one else, but scary me!

ABOUT THE AUTHOR

Kirsten Hall was born in New York City. While she was still in high school, she published her first book for children, *Bunny, Bunny*. Since then, she has written and published fifteen other children's books. Currently, Hall attends Connecticut College in new London, Connecticut, where she studies art, French, creative writing, and child development. She is not yet sure what her plans for the future will be—except that they will definitely include continuing to write for children.

ABOUT THE ILLUSTRATOR

John Magine was born in Evanston, Illinois. His career in commercial art and advertising brought him to California, where he now lives with his cat, Bogart, in San Rafael. Magine enjoys running, and mountain biking on Mount Tam. He also has a private pilot's license.